LiTTLe MiSS POKeY OaKS

CARTOON NETWORK™

by Howie Dewin
Based on
"THE POWERPUFF GIRLS,"
as created by Craig McCracken

SCHOLASTIC INC.

New York   Toronto   London   Auckland   Sydney
Mexico City   New Delhi   Hong Kong   Buenos Aires

ISBN 0-439-33214-1

Cover and interior illustrations by Mark Marderosian

Designed by Peter Koblish

12 11 10 9 8 7 6 5 4 3 2 1   2 3 4 5 6 7/0

Printed in the U.S.A.
First Scholastic printing, August 2002

The city of Townsville . . . and it's a beautiful day. The birds are singing. The sky is blue. Folks on the street can't stop smiling at one another. It's a perfect day, and the kids at Pokey Oaks Kindergarten think it's double perfect because it's also Friday!

"Hooray for Friday! Hooray for Friday!" A group of kids was chanting and stamping their feet. Ms. Keane had been called out of the classroom, and the

kindergartners were not behaving themselves.

"Blast off!" shouted Elmer Sglue. He
shot a paper airplane across the room. It
passed several spitballs along the way.
One of the spitballs hit Princess Mor-
bucks right in the head.

"That's disgusting!" cried Princess as
she pulled the spitball from her hair.

"Good thing she found it right away,"
Buttercup muttered to Bubbles. "A spitball could get lost in that hair forever!"

"I heard that!" Princess roared at Buttercup.

"So? You wanna make something of
it?" said Buttercup, standing up.

"Buttercup! Just ignore her," Blossom
said.

"Ignore me?" Princess screamed.

"Ignore me? Nobody ignores Princess and gets away with it!"

"Hey, everyone!" Blossom shouted. The children turned their attention to her. "We shouldn't misbehave just because Ms. Keane got called out of the classroom."

"There she goes!" sneered Princess. "Little-Miss-I'm-in-Charge-Just-Because-I-Have-Superpowers Powerpuff Girl!"

Just then, Ms. Keane returned. "Princess! Please find your seat. I'm disappointed to see you misbehave just because I got called out of the classroom."

The rest of the children stared innocently at Princess. Elmer Sglue nodded in agreement with Ms. Keane.

"I HATE The Powerpuff Girls," muttered Princess.

"Now, boys and girls, I know everyone is ready to have a wonderful weekend in the sun, but I have an announcement," Ms. Keane said.

An excited chatter rose up from the students.

"The Mayor has just informed me that the annual Little Miss Pokey Oaks Pageant will be held this

Monday," Ms. Keane continued. "All the girls in this class are automatically entered!"

The excited chatter swelled into a squeal.

"The competition will have three parts — fancy dress, interview, and a talent contest. Everyone will compete in all three areas."

"What's the big deal?" snarled Princess. "What does Little Miss Pokey Oaks get to do, anyway?"

The rest of the girls gasped.

"For your information," Blossom said, looking at Princess with disdain, "the title of Little Miss Pokey Oaks is a supreme honor! The winner represents Pokey Oaks Kindergarten at the Memorial Day parade."

"And she gets to wear a sparkly crown and a beautiful glittery dress and carry a wand with a silver star on the end!" Bubbles exclaimed.

The girls in the class giggled and whispered to one another.

"You all have the weekend to prepare for the competition," Ms. Keane continued. "And boys, don't forget, you will march along with the float. Good luck to everyone and I'll see you on Monday!"

The bell rang, but it was drowned out by the shouts and screams of excited kids.

Robin Schneider rushed up to Buttercup and Bubbles. "I can't wait to see what everyone does for the talent show! I think I might tap-dance!" Her blue eyes danced merrily.

"I'm going to be a clown," announced Julie Bean. She grabbed her bright red hair and held it straight out to the sides.

"I'm gonna kick some butt!" Buttercup declared.

"Kicking butt is not a talent," Princess hissed.

"It is the way I do it," Buttercup replied.

"What are you going to do, Mary?" Blossom asked her friend Mary Thompson.

"Oh, I'd rather just watch. I don't think I'll compete," Mary said. She was a little shy sometimes.

"But it's the very best part of being in kindergarten," Bubbles protested.

"Personally, I think it's bad for our self-image as girls," Blossom said. "These kinds of pageants send the wrong message about what's important. But it *is* a supreme honor, and that's what's *most* important."

"What's important is to kick butt!" Buttercup said.

"But it would be fun to win," Blossom admitted.

"I would love to wear that beautiful sparkly dress," Bubbles said dreamily.

"Well," said Princess, stamping toward the classroom door, "I think it's stupid. BUT if all three of *you* want it so bad, then I'm going to win it!" She stuck her nose up in the air. "Just you wait and see!"

Chapter 2

"Prin-c-c-e-s-s-s-s-s," Buttercup hissed. "I will crush her!"

"Oh, she's not going to win," Blossom said confidently. "Not with me in the show. As a natural-born leader, I will lead the way."

The Girls were heading home from school. They were darting back and forth as they spoke. Nothing could dampen their excitement — not even Princess.

"Well, excuse me," Buttercup said.

"But you're not the only superhero who's going to compete, you know! Besides, I thought you didn't approve of pageants."

"I don't," Blossom said. "And as soon as I become Little Miss Pokey Oaks, I will work very hard to make sure there's never another one! Besides, I thought YOU would think this was a stupid waste of time."

"It is," said Buttercup. "But I never miss a chance to kick butt, which is exactly what I'm going to do."

"You'll kick Princess's butt, but you won't kick *mine*." Blossom's cheeks were turning almost as red as her hair.

"But you're not going to be Little Miss

Pokey Oaks!" Bubbles protested. "I want to wear that sparkly crown. It will look bee-you-ti-ful on me."

"You're both gonna lose," Buttercup said. "I'm going to be the fiercest kick-boxing Little Miss Pokey Oaks this town has ever seen!"

"I'm going to make the most beautiful costume anyone has ever seen," said Bubbles. She was lost in the world of her imagination.

"It's more than just dressing up and being beautiful," Blossom reminded her sister.

"I know that," Bubbles said, snapping back to reality. "I'm going to sing! I will sing a pretty song written by *me*. I will wear my beautiful costume and sing my beautiful song!"

"Oh, brother!" Buttercup rolled her eyes.

"Well, it's better than kickboxing with a nasty old pair of boxing gloves! That's not very pretty," Bubbles declared.

"It won't matter what kind of gloves she wears," Blossom said. "I'm going to recite Shakespeare. There isn't another kindergartner at Pokey Oaks who can do that!"

"Lucky for us," Buttercup said under her breath.

"Oh, yeah?" Blossom challenged her. They were almost home by now.

"Yeah!" Buttercup replied.

"Yeah!" Bubbles joined in.

Just then, the Professor opened the door.

"Wanna prove it?" Blossom challenged.

"Any day!" Buttercup answered.

"Girls! Girls! What's going on?" the Professor asked.

"I'm going to be Little Miss Pokey Oaks!" Bubbles cried as she flew over to the Professor.

"'Fraid not!" Buttercup said scornfully, following her.

The three Girls were all talking at

once. Since they kept interrupting one another, it was a few minutes before the Professor understood what was going on. At last, he managed to get a word in edgewise. "Well now, Girls, I think this calls for a little kindness and generosity. The three of you should root for one another."

The Girls were silent. For a minute, they looked ashamed of themselves. But then Buttercup spoke up.

"Yeah, right!" she snapped. She zoomed up to the bedroom.

"I don't think so, Professor," Bubbles answered.

"I'll root for them to do well and for me to do better," Blossom told him. Then she followed her sisters upstairs.

"Oh, dear," muttered the Professor. He shook his head. Even though the door to the Girls' bedroom was closed, he could hear them shouting at one another.

It was going to be a long weekend.

With all the arguing, no one heard the sound of a cell phone beeping in the bushes. Crouched in the thick hedges outside The Powerpuff Girls' house, Princess was dialing her phone. She'd secretly followed the Girls home and heard everything they'd said.

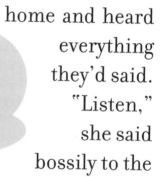

"Listen," she said bossily to the person on the other end of the phone. "Do exactly what I say."

There was a pause.

"Because I said so!" Princess snapped.

"And I'm paying you good money to do what I say! Now, go to the grocery store and start destroying everything. Don't stop until The Powerpuff Girls show up!"

Princess hung up the phone. "Shakespeare! Singing! Kickboxing!" she hissed. "I'll keep them so busy all weekend, they won't be able to do anything but fight evil." She giggled evilly. "As of this moment, those silly Gangreen Gangsters are doing my bidding! There will be no rest for you this weekend, Powerpuff Girls!"

Oh, dear. Sister fighting sister. Will Townsville survive the Little Miss Pokey Oaks contest?

chapter 3

B-r-r-r-r-r-ingggg!

"To be or not to be," Blossom quoted loudly.

"Would you please practice that somewhere else?" Buttercup yelled at her. "Like the North Pole!"

B-r-r-r-r-r-inggggg!

"Here she is," Bubbles sang, "Little Miss Pokey Oaks . . . "

B-r-r-r-r-r-ingggggg!

The Professor appeared in the doorway of the Girls' room. "Girls! The hotline is ringing!" he shouted over the ruckus.

"Oh," the Girls said in unison. The room went quiet.

B-r-r-r-r-r-ingggggg!

Blossom picked up the hotline. "Hello?" She listened for a minute. "We'll be right there!" She hung up the phone and turned to her sisters. "The grocery store, Girls. It's the Gangreen Gang!"

The three sisters zoomed out of their room without delay. But as they flew toward the center of town, they continued bickering.

"I can't believe they chose *now* to destroy the grocery store. I'm gonna mangle those Gangreen Gangsters. I don't have time for this," Buttercup snarled.

"That's the problem with beauty pageants," Blossom lectured. "Suddenly, you care more about winning a crown than you do about stopping crime."

"And you don't?" Bubbles asked her sister.

"Certainly not!" Blossom answered. "My most important job is fighting crime. That's what I'll tell all my fans when I accept the Little Miss Pokey Oaks crown."

"There they are!" Bubbles said, pointing down at the ground.

The Gangreen Gang was making a real mess. The street in front of the grocery store was covered with lots of different kinds of smashed fruits and vegetables.

"What's wrong with them?" Buttercup growled.

"What's the point of this?" Bubbles shouted.

Buttercup didn't wait for an answer. She aimed herself directly at Ace and took off. Before the leader of the Gang even knew The Powerpuff Girls were on the scene, he was flat on his back.

Blossom knocked out Big Billy with one zap of an eye beam. Bubbles threw three kicks and four punches, and the rest of the Gang was history.

As the people of Townsville cheered, the Girls kicked the Gang to the curb.

"Now behave yourselves!" Blossom commanded. "I don't have time for this kind of nonsense right now!"

The pile of villains moaned as the Girls streaked back toward home. Around the corner, Princess watched them disappear into the sky. Then she ducked down an alley and dialed her cell phone.

Fifteen minutes later, The Powerpuff Girls' hotline rang again.

B-r-r-r-r-r-inggggg!

B-r-r-r-r-r-inggggg!

"Oh, for Pete's sake! Hello? Yes, Mayor. We'll be right there." Blossom hung up the phone. "Bubbles! Buttercup! It's the Amoeba Boys! They're at the movie theater and they're standing in front of the screen blocking the picture."

"Oh, come on!" Buttercup complained. "They're so stupid. Can't someone else deal with them?"

Blossom glared at her sister, then zoomed out her bedroom window. Her sisters followed, though Buttercup looked unhappy about it.

It took no time at all to rid the theater of the hopeless Amoeba Boys. "Move your sorry nuclei," Buttercup threatened, "or I'll blast you off the planet!" She charged them, but they fled in fear. The movie audience cheered.

Sitting in the back of the dark, crowded theater, Princess watched with satisfaction. She smirked and dialed another number on her phone.

That afternoon, the hotline seemed to ring every five minutes. No sooner would the Girls stop one crime than another would be committed. And each battle was sillier than the one before. It was as if all the villains in Townsville had lost

their minds. They were committing crimes so stupid it seemed like they *wanted* to get caught.

At nightfall, Fuzzy Lumpkins showed up at the Townsville bowling alley. He started throwing bowling balls in reverse, back at the bowlers. The Girls zipped down the lane and sent Fuzzy running back to his cabin with a couple of power punches and a sonic slap.

The Girls dropped to the bowling alley floor and looked at one another. They were worn out.

"I'm so tired," said Bubbles, yawning. "I know I should work on my song but . . ."

"I know. I was going to work on my kickboxing routine, but now I just want to catch some zzzz's," Buttercup replied, rubbing her eyes.

"Something strange is going on," Blossom said. "We haven't fought a single real battle, and I'm whipped."

"It's almost as if someone is trying to distract us on purpose," Bubbles said.

It was the first time the Girls had agreed with one another all day.

"I bet I know who it is!" Blossom declared.

"Princess!" Buttercup said.

Bubbles lost it. "That's it!" she screeched. "An entire day of rehearsing my big number gone! I'm not answering another call!"

Hiding behind the bowling shoe rack, Princess narrowed her eyes. "Then I guess it's time for Plan B!" she whispered. She dialed another number on her cell phone. "Proceed with Plan B," she commanded. "And make it snappy!"

Watch out, Girls! Princess is on a hot streak and she's shootin' for a strike. If you're not careful, you'll wind up in the gutter — and Princess will be Little Miss Pokey Oaks!

Chapter 4

The next morning, the Girls woke up with a start. The Professor was calling them from downstairs. "Oh, Girls! I have a surprise for you!"

The Girls stirred in their bed.

"Surprise?" Bubbles groaned.

"It's probably another trick." Buttercup yawned.

"The Mayor sent you each a present," the Professor called.

"The Mayor?" Blossom perked up.

"Present?" Bubbles shot out of bed.

"Cool," Buttercup said, zipping down-stairs ahead of her sisters.

Three beautifully wrapped presents sat by the front door.

The Professor read from a card, *"For The Powerpuff Girls. On behalf of the citizens of Townsville, thank you for your hard work. We're rooting for all of you. Good luck tomor-row! From the Mayor."* There were a few

words spelled wrong on the card, but the Girls didn't worry about that. The Mayor wasn't a great speller.

"Oooooh!" Bubbles squealed. She and her sisters dove on the packages and ripped away the ribbon and wrapping paper. They threw off the box tops and held up their gifts.

"Oooh! It's *beeeee-you-ti-ful!*" Bubbles exclaimed as she gazed at a silky new dress. "It's just what I imagined!"

"These rock!" Butter-cup declared. She held up a shiny new pair of leather boxing gloves. Her name was embroidered across both gloves.

"Look at this," Blossom said quietly. She was in awe. She held up a beautiful leather-bound book. The engraved gold lettering on top said *Shakespeare's Greatest Hits.* "I've never had a book this nice before."

The Professor smiled at the Girls. "Well, I hope this means you can stop fighting and get to work."

"Absolutely!" Blossom declared. She settled into the couch and began to read.

"You bet," said Buttercup, pulling on her gloves.

Bubbles just giggled and flew upstairs with her new dress.

"Thank goodness," the Professor muttered to himself.

He headed off to his laboratory. Blossom, Bubbles, and Buttercup started rehearsing their acts. The house was finally quiet.

Outside the house, Princess peeked through the living room window.

"I'm a genius," she declared. "Who's a better Little Miss Pokey Oaks than me?" The spoiled troublemaker cackled quietly to herself, then hurried away from the house.

Inside the house, the day slipped by in silence.

Blossom read her new book cover to cover. She found the perfect piece to recite in the pageant. But before she could memorize it, she fell into a deep sleep on the couch.

In the kitchen, Buttercup cleared everything off the floor to give herself more space. Then she created an awesome kickboxing display. She worked all day until she was so tired she had to sit down to rest. A minute later, she was fast asleep on the floor.

Bubbles locked herself in the Girls' bedroom and finished writing her song. Then she put on her beautiful new dress and practiced singing it. When she got too tired to stand up, she lay down on her bed and went over the song in her head. She was asleep before she got through the first verse.

The Professor was very busy with a new invention. In fact, he was so involved in his project that he lost track of time.

The Girls usually pulled him away from his work when it was time for dinner. But today, the Girls were just as busy as the Professor. The house was completely quiet. Then —

The next morning!
"AAAAAAUUUUUUGGGGGHHH!"
The scream came from the Girls' bedroom. The Professor, who had dozed off in his lab, was startled awake. He ran upstairs and met Buttercup on the way.

"It's Bubbles, Professor!" Buttercup shouted.

The Professor swung open the bedroom door. Inside, Bubbles

was dashing around the room, jumping up and down like a monkey.

"What is it? What's wrong?" the Professor asked. He tried to catch up with her.

"I'm — all — AAAAUUUUGGGHHH!"

Bubbles could barely speak, she was so busy scratching herself.

"Itchy!" she screamed. "My dress is all — AUUUUGGGHHH!"

"I'll help you get it off," Buttercup said. She tried to pull off her gloves so she could help with the dress, but they wouldn't budge.

"Hey!" Buttercup said. She pulled again. "I can't get these off!"

Bubbles

finally pulled her dress off. She was a mess of itchy hives. She put on a bathrobe and then yanked at her sister's gloves. The Professor tried pulling, too. The gloves wouldn't move an inch.

"I think they're glued on!" Buttercup cried.

"AAAAAUUUUGGGGHHH!" Bubbles was still itching all over.

"Where's Blossom?" the Professor suddenly asked. It wasn't like the red-headed Powerpuff Girl to ignore her sisters' plight.

Bubbles and Buttercup blinked, then started to panic. They all rushed downstairs.

Blossom was sound asleep on the couch. Buttercup gave her a shake.

"Wake up! We've got trouble!" Buttercup shouted to her sister. But Blossom didn't move.

"AAAAAUUUUUGGGGGHHHH!"

Even Bubbles's shouts didn't wake her sister.

Buttercup examined the book in Blossom's lap. It was covered in a fine dust.

"Sleeping powder!" Buttercup declared.

"And my dress was doused in scratching powder!" Bubbles cried as she continued to scratch.

"And," added the Professor, "I bet there's some industrial-strength glue inside Buttercup's gloves."

Buttercup zoomed over to the table by the front door and

stared at the card that came with the gifts. She tried to pick it up, but couldn't. Her gloves were too clumsy. "Somebody open this card and show it to me!"

Bubbles wriggled over and held up the card.

Buttercup nodded. "That's not the Mayor's handwriting! We've been duped again!"

Bubbles began to sob. "And the pageant starts in two hours!"

"PRINCESS!" Buttercup roared.

Oh, no! Is Princess really going to beat The Powerpuff Girls? Bubbles? Buttercup? Blossom? Wake up, Blossom!

Chapter 5

"Help me get her into the shower!" Buttercup instructed Bubbles and the Professor. Buttercup put a clumsy boxing-gloved arm around Blossom and pulled her up. Blossom stayed asleep.

"I've got her. Start the shower," the Professor said as he carried Blossom upstairs.

Bubbles got the calamine lotion out of the cabinet. She covered her whole body with the pink lotion.

"Nice look," Buttercup said, smirking. Bubbles was covered in pink streaks and spots.

"I don't care as long as it stops the itching," Bubbles said sadly.

"Hey! Wha —? Cut it out!" Blossom sputtered from inside the shower. "What's going on?" She jumped out of the shower.

"You wouldn't wake up," Bubbles told Blossom.

"How come you're all pink?" she asked Bubbles.

"Never mind that," Buttercup snapped. "We've got work to do!" Buttercup tried to hand Blossom a towel, but it was impossible with her boxing gloves on.

"What's going on? What time is it?" Blossom asked.

Buttercup flew out of the bathroom. "We'll explain on the way to school. We're late! Let's go!"

"I can't go like this!" Bubbles whimpered.

"School?" Blossom asked, rubbing the sleep from her eyes.

"We have to tell Ms. Keane we're not competing . . . and we also have to kick Princess's butt!" Buttercup growled.

"Okaaaay . . . " Blossom had drifted off to sleep again.

"H-H-H-H-H-E-E-E-E-E-Y-Y-Y!" Buttercup shouted into her ear.

Blossom jerked awake. "WHAT?!" she cried.

"Follow me!"

The Girls flew out the door, but they were not their usual speedy selves. Bubbles's scratching kept sending her off course. Buttercup's gloves were throwing her off balance. She couldn't get above the treetops. And Blossom kept stalling in midair to sleep.

It took so long to get to school that by the time they arrived the pageant was about to begin.

"I'll explain everything to Ms. Keane," Blossom said. Then she fell asleep again.

Bubbles wanted to talk to Ms. Keane,

but she was in the middle of another itching attack.

At that very moment, Princess appeared. She was wearing the most beautiful dress Bubbles had ever seen. It was made of a fancy, shiny fabric that seemed to change color when she moved. And it was decorated with beautiful velvet ribbon.

Bubbles opened her mouth to give Princess a piece of her mind, but no words came out. "AAAAAUUUUU-UGGGGGHHHHHH!" was all she could shout.

"Nice makeup," Princess answered, turning up her nose.

"You won't get away with this, Princess!" Buttercup spat. She tried to throw Princess to the floor, but the gloves made it difficult for her to fly. So instead of zooming right into Princess's face, Buttercup zoomed right into Princess's kneecaps.

Princess easily dodged the attack. "Looks like I *have* gotten away with it," she said, laughing loudly. "Just wait until you see my talent act! Powerpuff, schmowerpuff!" Princess flounced away, giving the slumbering Blossom a little shove as she went. Blossom toppled over.

Tears ran down Bubbles's face. "I re-e-e-a-a-ally wanted to be Little Miss Pokey Oaks!"

"We're The Powerpuff Girls!" Buttercup said in a low but strong voice. "We're go-ing to compete

no matter what! It's the only way we can keep Princess from becoming Little Miss Pokey Oaks."

"How?" Blossom said sleepily, waking up for a moment. "We're not going to win. Not now."

"Maybe not, but if we don't at least compete, we won't be backstage. And if we're not backstage, we won't be able to sabotage Princess and keep her from stealing the crown!" Buttercup declared.

"That's not very good sportsman-ship." Blossom yawned.

"This isn't sports," Buttercup said, narrowing her eyes. "This is war!"

Thatta girl, Buttercup! Give it the ol' superhero try! We're counting on you!

chapter 6

"Ladies and gentlemen, welcome to the annual Little Miss Pokey Oaks Pageant!"

The crowd cheered as Ms. Keane began the show. The Girls stood backstage, miserable. They didn't know how to stop Princess, but they knew they had to.

"If I could stay awake, I would be really, really mad," Blossom muttered. "This is so unfair . . . sscchhnnoozzz."

"Hey!" Buttercup poked Blossom. She

only meant to nudge her, but with the boxing gloves on she actually sent Blossom tumbling head over heels.

"Buttercup!" Bubbles exclaimed.

"It was an accident," Buttercup apologized.

"I'm awake, I'm awake," Blossom sputtered.

Their classmates filed past them. All the other girls were dressed in beautiful gowns. The Girls looked at themselves. Blossom was in the same dress she'd worn the day before and then slept in. Buttercup was in an old workout dress. But Bubbles was in the worst shape. She was still in her bathrobe and covered in calamine. Tears ran down her face.

"Powerpuff Girls!" Ms. Keane called out. "Find your place in line!" She was too busy to notice the Girls weren't dressed properly.

"This stinks," Buttercup said as she fell into line. She pulled the half-asleep Blossom behind her. Bubbles followed, knowing she had no choice.

As the Girls walked on-stage, the crowd cheered for the famous Powerpuff Girls. But then, as the audience got a full look at the Girls, a ripple of laughter spread across the room. Buttercup turned bright red in anger. Bubbles hid her face in the collar of her dress. Blossom just snored.

As the Girls hurried offstage again, the audience's cheers grew louder. The Girls turned back to see Princess standing center stage. She was wearing the gorgeous dress they'd seen before, but now she also wore a long sequined cape. It was so enormous it covered the whole stage. The audience loved her.

"What do we do? What do we do?" Bubbles cried.

"We'll get her during the interviews," Buttercup said.

Blossom nodded slightly, then shook her head to keep herself awake.

But things only got worse during the interviews.

"What one thing is the most important to you?" Ms. Keane asked Buttercup.

Buttercup cleared her throat and began to talk about fighting for justice and the importance of fairness. But then she started thinking about Princess and how unfair she'd been, and she got really angry. Suddenly, she was shouting about kicking butt. Then, as she gestured with one of her arms, she accidentally slugged Ms. Keane with her boxing glove. As soon as she was sure Ms. Keane was okay, Buttercup ran offstage. The audience sat in shocked silence.

Princess was next, and the crowd roared with approval.

"This is hopeless!" Blossom said, a little more awake now.

"It was an accident!" Buttercup said.

"Forget it," Bubbles said sadly. "Let's just go home."

"No!" Buttercup refused to give up. "Bubbles, you have to sing your song. The

Powerpuff Girls cannot be the laughing-stock of the Little Miss Pokey Oaks Pageant."

Bubbles quietly agreed. She walked on-stage, trying to look beautiful. She smiled sweetly at the crowd, and they cheered.

Their applause grew louder after she'd sung the first few lines of her song. Blossom and Butter-cup clapped in the wings.

But then, Bubbles seemed to forget one word, then another. It was hard to understand what she was saying. As Buttercup and Blossom watched in horror, Bubbles started pulling on her tongue.

"Oh, no," Buttercup moaned. "Her tongue is itching!"

"AAAAAUUUUUGGGGHHHH!" Bubbles screeched. She scratched madly at her tongue, then flew offstage in shame. She was hiding in a corner when her sisters found her.

"Now Princess is going to be Little Miss Pokey Oaks for sure," Bubbles cried.

"It's okay." Blossom tried to sound cheerful. "You were great until that tongue thing started."

Bubbles cried harder. But her sobs were nothing compared to the explosion of applause that came from the audience. The Powerpuff Girls flew to the curtain's edge to watch what was happening. They couldn't believe their eyes.

In the center spotlight, Princess sat high atop a stunning horse. She wore a bright yellow cowgirl outfit covered with sequins and fringe.

"Wow," said Bubbles. "Is that a real horse?"

"I don't think so," Blossom answered. "Look at its eyes. They're electric." Blossom pointed to two little blue bulbs shining where the horse's eyes should have been.

"She bought some kind of superpowered mechanical horse just for the pageant?!" Buttercup couldn't believe it.

Just then, Princess pulled out a lasso. She held it in the air. The lasso started twirling itself. It lit up with brightly colored sparks. The crowd roared.

Then she pulled two toy pistols from her

holsters. She shot them into the air and fireworks exploded above her head.

"That's not talent," Blossom said. "That's just an expensive toy."

"But you have to admit it's cool," Buttercup said in defeat. "That's all the audience cares about."

A high-pitched screech pulled the Girls' attention back to the stage. The horse was up on its hind legs, and Princess was on the floor. Screams from the audience filled the air.

"What happened?" Bubbles asked.

The horse's eyes were no longer blue. They were flashing an angry red. Suddenly, the horse was running wild across the stage. When it got near the front it leaped right into the audience. People ran in all directions, screaming and shouting.

"I think Princess's horse blew a fuse!" Buttercup said. She couldn't help smiling a little bit.

"We'd better do something," Blossom shouted.

"Let's go!" Bubbles yelled.

"Heigh-ho, Silver!" said Buttercup. "Away!"

chapter 7

"Yeeeee-haaaaw!" cried Buttercup. She was flying better than she had all day. She felt great. She tore through the air at top speed, heading straight for the wild electric horse. She aimed her boxing gloves at the horse and slammed right into it.

The horse went sailing through the air, throwing dangerous sparks and fireworks in every direction. Fires began to appear throughout the auditorium. Bubbles zoomed over and put out every ember with her extra calamine lotion.

Just as the horse was about to land on a group of terrified people, Blossom woke up. At the speed of light, she flew toward the horse and grabbed it before it landed. The horse kicked and screeched while Blossom pulled on the reins.

"Bubbles! Buttercup!" Blossom called.

Bubbles grabbed the horse's tail while Buttercup pushed up with her boxing gloves and forced the horse high above the crowd. Together, the Girls flew the horse out of the auditorium and dumped it into a nearby pool.

Outside the auditorium, the audience gathered to watch the end of the battle. In the pool, the horse sputtered and sparked

a few more times. Finally, it stopped moving. The audience exploded with the loudest cheer ever.

"Little Miss Pokey Oaks! Little Miss Pokey Oaks! Little Miss Pokey Oaks!" they chanted. They wouldn't stop until each of The Powerpuff Girls was wearing a shiny new tiara.

Blossom raised an arm to quiet the

crowd. "My sisters and I want to thank you for this honor, but it isn't right to exclude our friends. We cannot represent Pokey Oaks unless all our friends are allowed to ride on the float with us. We are all Little Miss Pokey Oaks!"

The roar of the crowd was deafening.

"That's a wonderful idea, Blossom," Ms. Keane said. "We'll all ride on the float together!"

The next day!

It was a perfect Memorial Day in Townsville. The sun was shining and all the girls of Pokey Oaks proudly represented their school on the Pokey Oaks float. Everyone had a tiara and a beautiful, glittering wand.

"This is perfect," sighed Bubbles, waving to the crowd.

"I know," agreed Blossom. "The parade has gone off without a hitch!"

"Well," said Buttercup, "actually, there's one hitch." She pointed to the front of the float. Someone in a silly horse costume was hitched up and pulling the float down Main Street.